I0640938

Firebrand Firestorm

The Ancestors of Bjorn Esterday

Volume 10

Suspicion

June 1770

Wynter Sommers

Wynter Sommers

Published by Pure Force Enterprises, Inc.
California, USA
Since 2002

INGRAM
INGRAM® Distribution

ISBN-13: 978-1-7184-0022-1
ISBN-10: 1-7184-0022-5

DEDICATION

To those who feel strongly about truth, justice, and the integrity of America; your honorable actions make us proud. To those who wonder if their daily choices matter; your small decisions impact generations to come. To those everyday people who don't think they have what it takes; when you strive for extraordinary things, the impossible becomes reality. Your dreams today become our future tomorrow. Thank you for everything you do.

Bjorn Esterday
Was Not Born Yesterday
Series

Firebrand (15 Volumes+Conversation Station Book)
Edges (9 Stories +Conversation Station Book)
Gone (18 Stories + Conversation Station Book)

Bjorn EDGES Series
EDGES Book 1-Swift Encounter
EDGES Book 2-Rousing Attack
EDGES Book 3-One Foot Under
EDGES Book 4-Earthshake
EDGES Book 5-Broken String
EDGES Book 6-Key Witness
EDGES Book 7-Who is She?
EDGES Book 8-Vanish
EDGES Book 9-Chase or Die

Bjorn Series Alternate Reading Plan

1st	Edges Book 1		22nd	Gone Book 10
2nd	Edges Book 2		23rd	Firebrand Vol 9
3rd	Gone Book 1		24rd	Gone Book 11
4th	Firebrand Vol 1		25th	Firebrand Vol 10
5th	Edges Book 3		26th	Gone Book 12
6th	Firebrand Vol 2		27th	Gone Book 13
7th	Gone Book 2		28th	Firebrand Vol 11
8th	Gone Book 3		29th	Gone Book 14
9th	Firebrand Vol 3		30th	Firebrand Vol 12
10th	Gone Book 4		31st	Gone Book 15
11th	Firebrand Vol 4		32nd	Firebrand Vol 13
12th	Gone Book 5		33rd	Gone Book 16
13th	Gone Book 6		34th	Firebrand Vol 14
14th	Edges Book 4		35th	Gone Book 17
15th	Firebrand Vol 5		36th	Firebrand Vol15 (End)
16th	Gone Book 7		37th	Gone Book 18 (End)
17th	Firebrand Vol 6		38th	Edges Book 5
18th	Gone Book 8		39th	Edges Book 6
19th	Firebrand Vol 7		40th	Edges Book 7
20th	Gone Book 9		41st	Edges Book 8
21st	Firebrand Vol 8		42nd	Edges Book 9(End)

ACKNOWLEDGMENTS

We acknowledge those who actively build peace. We acknowledge all the selfless talent which contributed to creating meaningful tokens of consideration and sharing. We acknowledge that every person has a daily choice of right or wrong... and we thank you for choosing the right, good, honorable path filled with integrity because that is the difficult and brave path. Small choices today become lasting monuments of loving hope tomorrow.

CONTENTS

0 PREFACE

Later in this account, we discover what transpires next. Last time, the magistrate changed directions. Button was asked what he was prepared to do to defend this concept of 'freedom'. Is Button just voicing a popular opinion? Or is he willing to underscore that he means what he says? Is he ready to abandon what may have happened to his wife? Does he continue onward with single focused disinterest about the plight of his wife and unborn child? Should he assume they are dead, grieve, and move on? Or should he keep hoping and never give up searching for Polly, his wife and their child?

1 CHAPTER 88: (JUNE 1776) Barn Through the Looking Glass

The unassuming barn, which contained a volatile group of participants debating about the value of attempting yet another colonial unification, stood outlined in shadow against the fading rays of a setting sun. Dark clouds clustered overhead. Gusts of wind licked up bits of straw from the tall haystacks dotting the field around the barn.

Sheep and lambs were aimlessly wandering about far way in the neighbor's field. Their occasional bleating echoed across the valley. Yet, a silent stray lamb had explored the haystacks

2

near the barn, and had developed a taste for the skirts of Jane Hargreaves' lady's maid, Silversmith.

Poor Silversmith was attempting to remain unseen as she strained to overhear the conversation of a small party of men just outside the barn. Silversmith had recognized Henry Mossop, the arrogant opera singer who performed at Lady Sarah Wilson's estate. Silversmith recognized him and did not know if he would recognize her, a servant. Silversmith opted to remain concealed behind the haystack.

Glancing over her shoulder, she now saw, in the distance, the stable boys on horseback riding right toward her on the path returning to the barn.

Some occupants of the concluded meeting, still talking as they waited within the barn, also noticed the approaching stable boys. Horses would have to eventually occupy the stalls inside the barn, displacing the meeting attendees.

Looking out through a knothole in one of the barn planks, one attendee suddenly realized their meeting had to disband immediately! The stable boys needed to get back to their duties before the winds turned into a storm.

Silversmith's eyes started to water as the wind whistled through holes in the wooden planks of the barn. Bits of hay and dust whipped around her, prompting her to sneeze, which she did, as softly as she could.

She froze. She hoped the men were too involved in their conversation to hear her.

Then she felt the cloud-like, slightly dirty wool of a young warm creature push against her ankles. She looked down to see a little lamb staring up at her.

Then, without breaking its hypnotic gaze, this tiny gentle baby creature started to chew on the hem of Silversmith's skirts. With one hand, silversmith tried to tug her skirts away, but the blank stare of the animal simply locked onto Silversmith as it kept a firm grip on her garment.

Silversmith continued to strain to overhear the conversations of these men nearby. They spoke freely when they thought they were not overheard.

"It is time to light the candle," Mossop announced plainly.

"Ah. Right. The signal. Will they see it?" The other man inquired, "Will the wind blow out the flame?" Silversmith glanced again at the now shadowy silhouettes of the stable boys approaching on horseback.

Looking down at the lamb, Silversmith kneeled and tried to push the baby lamb away with the palm of her hand. The lamb released the hem of her now torn garment, but it "baaah-ed".

Silversmith quickly shoved the hem of her skirt back in its mouth, and it resumed slowly chewing.

Silversmith shook her head and bit her lower lip.

"I heard something," One man announced.

"Farm animals," Another dismissed.

"Perhaps we spoke too freely and were overheard?" Henry Mossop, the opera singer, commented while putting his hand on what looked like the hilt of a knife.

"I shall investigate, Sir," The other uttered as he pivoted and took a step toward the haystack where silversmith hid.

One man looked back at the barn to ensure the doors remained shut while Henry Mossop turned toward the approaching stable boys.

Mossop continued with entitled officious orders, "We don't have time. Those boys will have to put the horses back inside the barn and our chance will have been lost. Quickly. Find whatever made that noise," the opera singer barked.

With a jolt, Silversmith yanked her skirt out of the mouth of the sheep and as last time, the lamb bleated more loudly. With the side of her ankle, Silversmith pushed the lamb to the edge of the haystack so it would be seen. The lamb stumbled into the clearing, still chewing the vestiges of a scrap of fabric from Silversmith's skirts. This time the lamb locked eyes with the approaching fellow.

The men didn't notice that the creature was chewing cloth.

Silversmith heard the Opera singer, Henry Mossop, exhale in relief and say, "I must be anxious. It's just a small lamb."

Silversmith heard one of the other men approach and pick up the lamb.

Luckily, the lamb must have swallowed the fabric it was chewing because the men did not make any comments about it.

"Dinner?" The man suggested to the lamb as he patted its head.

"Well done," Henry Mossop commended.

The man holding the lamb replied while now tucking the baby lamb under his arm, "Would you like it roasted with rosemary or thyme? After we light the candle, we can go to the other side of the field, and see if we can dig up some potatoes from this farmer's land? He won't miss a few."

"Don't sheepherders count all their sheep?" another asked.

He replied, "They won't miss one tiny lamb. The others are all the way over there."

Silversmith wondered at these men, expensively dressed in finery, yet relishing the thrill of a stolen meal. She concluded they steal because they feel entitled to. They harm innocents because they feel justified in fanning their power like the ornate tail feathers of a male peacock.

As the men came closer to her haystack, Silversmith quietly stepped around the haystack to always keep the pile of hay between her and these men.

But soon, there would be no place to hide as the stable boys were now getting even closer.

Silversmith reasoned if these wealthy men had no qualms about pilfering a lamb from a farmer who was kind enough to lend them his barn for a meeting, then they would have no compunctions about taking Silversmith herself to either sell or simply harm. She considered that her current predicament was beyond that of traditional job duties assigned to a typical Lady's Maid.

Additionally, Silversmith saw no way of escape because, should the stable boys, even nicely, ask if she were lost... then Henry Mossop's men would know she had overheard them and would take her forcibly.

The bang of the barn door opening startled Silversmith and the men. People hurried out quickly.

Silversmith held her breath as she tried not to sneeze again, and pushed her back into the haystack hoping to perhaps hide inside of it.

From the other side of the haystack, the side where the men were, she heard the clip clop of horses hooves and the sound of wooden wheels.

The carriage was driven around the haystack so the carriage door was in front of her, but the horses and Billy Dawes stopped inches away from where Henry Mossop and his two men stood.

Peter Timothy yelled clearly as he

opened the door of the carriage, "I say, my good men!" One startled cohort tried to hide the struggling lamb under his jacket.

Peter continued boldly with, "I seem to have lost my little lamb… have you seen her?" Peter asked, acting as if he did not notice the bulge beneath one man's coat.

Peter started to whistle for it, as if it had a name, "Raised to be a pet, you see… uh… Snowflake is her name…" Peter explained as he stood forcing the men to look at him and away from the carriage.

Billy Dawes squinted at Silversmith and jerked his head slightly.

Peter Timothy pulled out a shiny coin, "I was going to give a reward for finding her…" he held the coin up so it glinted in the fading light.

Billy Dawes spied Silversmith, again, wondered why she had not interpreted his look as an invitation to secretly enter the carriage. Although, this was not a rehearsed plan, and he could not look at her lest he reveal her hiding location, all he could think of doing was... just sit there and grimace.

"Oh!" One of Henry Mossop's men grunted, "I think I've found your precious pet," he smiled as he proudly proffered the lamb from under his lumpy jacket.

"That's her! That's my Snowflake!" Peter Timothy exclaimed as he held his arms out to accept the animal and pressed the coin into the man's hands.

Silversmith gingerly opened the door of the carriage a bit wider. As quietly as she could, she pushed both her hands down on the floor of the carriage to lift herself up and flatten herself onto the floor of the vehicle.

Here, she quietly lay, leaving the door ajar. Billy Dawes cleared his throat to alert Peter Timothy.

The stable boys were now upon the barn and, as expected, one shouted, "Who are ye? Lost? Collecting somebody?"

Billy simply nodded his head and shouted back, "My master's business is nearly done."

The head stable boy seemed to be satisfied with that comment and continued to walk toward the barn. Henry Mossop's expression darkened as he glanced at his pocket watch.

Peter Timothy, still clutching the frightened lamb hopped into the carriage, ignoring Silversmith on the floor.

As Peter Timothy closed the door after him with one hand, holding the lamb with the other, Billy Dawes snapped his reins and galloped off with his passengers safely within his carriage walls.

After Billy Dawes rode away, he thumped on the roof of his carriage to alert the occupants inside, it was safe for Silversmith to get up from the floor of the moving vehicle.

Billy slowed the horses but continued to move the carriage forward. Silversmith carefully looked back.

"That man," she shared with Peter Timothy and his new-found lamb, "...Henry Mossop... he said he had to light a candle. It looks as if he has done. What think you about that, sir?"

"A candle flame is small," Peter Timothy replied, "... but it is light enough to act as a signal if somebody were expecting it. Do you know what the signal was for, Silversmith?"

Back near the barn, the flickering flame was barely visible this far way, but one could see it if one knew where to look.

Silversmith replied, "Mr. Timothy, I do not know who would be watching for a candle flame on this windy night. I do not know what it means." She reached out to pet the lamb and added, "But, thank you, Mr. Timothy, for collecting me. I was so scared... they may slaughter me as they had planned to with that lamb there."

Peter Timothy replied, "With Mr. Dawes' spyglass, we could see this small creature nearly succeed in revealing your hiding spot. You know, he kept an eye on you the entire time, Silversmith."

"Billy Dawes?" Silversmith asked, looking down.

"Yes. He seems very devoted to... keeping you safe," Peter Timothy smiled.

Blushing and unable to respond to the implication that Mr. Dawes held Silversmith in high regard, Silversmith changed the subject by saying, "It was a brilliant plan to buy the lamb... Even though they were right. The farmer wouldn't have noticed one lamb missing..."

"Miss Silversmith," Peter started, "any shepherd knows each and every one of his flock. This lamb would have been missed, I assure you. These are fine wool sheep. Soft Alpaca. They are raised to be sheered, not to be food. Men like that only respond to gold and fear. I had to buy her and..." Peter thumped the roof of the carriage as they seemed to leave one property and approach the neighboring property... the field with a multitude of bleating sheep roaming about the soft green pastures.

The carriage slowed to a stop.

Peter Timothy opened the door and hopped out with the lamb tucked under his arm. His leather boots crunched against the gravel on the road as he approached the fence post marker indicating a new property.

In the distance, he heard the bleating of the sheep. Gently, Peter Timothy, son to authoress and publisher Elizabeth Timothy, placed the lamb on the ground on the other side of the fence.

Once the tiny wool bundle touched the soft green blades of grass, its ears perked up in response to the bleating.

It bleated a high pitch reply and then scampered toward the flock.

Peter Timothy walked quickly to the carriage, swung himself back in and closed the door behind him, thumping the roof to alert Billy Dawes to keep moving.

"And? As you were saying?" Silversmith asked as she now felt safe enough to sit upon the seat opposite Peter Timothy.

"And free that little lamb to give her another chance at life... and return her to her flock..." Peter Timothy smiled as he continued, "That little creature may be cold for a night, but won't become anybody's dinner. The shepherd will keep that lamb close by so it doesn't wander off, again. I bought the lamb so I could free it. "

"As you freed me when you didn't have to?" Silversmith said, "When you and Mr. Dawes could have left me there to whatever my fate might have been?"

Peter pondered a moment before replying to Silversmith, "As we must all work together to ensure all people remain free. We must stymie evil impulses in others, so ordinary people can safely embrace the opportunity to do great things."

"Oh," Silversmith shook her head as they bumped along the dirt road, "I am but a maid, Sir. A lady's maid who can read and write and arrange my mistress' hair in the latest fashion, but I fear I can do nothing to ensure the safety or freedom of others... let alone do great things..."

"Do you not realize, Miss Silversmith, that you already have?" Peter Timothy explained tenderly, "Pray, tell me what you overheard and I'll wager the information is more valuable than you realize..."

2 CHAPTER 89: (JUNE 1776) Still In the Carriage

After being lulled to sleep by the gentle sway of the carriage rhythmically rolling wooden wheels along the dirt road, a loud noise awoke all the carriage occupants travelling north to the Meeting Town. Jane awoke first, then Eliza and of course their two Canada-bound travelling companions, Eunice and her son TallMan.

"What was that?" Eliza Lucas exclaimed, her voice laced with panic.

Once all the occupants were fully awake, there came another loud bang from a different direction. From atop the carriage, the occupants could hear the driver attempting to calm the now agitated horses with a loud slow, "Whoa…whooooooaaaaah…"

Jane reached for the door and TallMan placed his hand on hers to stop her. TallMan advised, "Not wise. That noise sounds like firearm rapports." He advised. Then another BANG BANG sounded.

"Why would anybody shoot at us?" Eliza asked as she nervously fingered her brooch, then took it off and placed it safely inside her bodice where it could not be seen.

Jane looked at her own person. She was not wearing any jewelry. She had only her cosmetics case. She had nothing of value to steal save the coins she brought with her to settle her maid's hotel debt… and that was no fortune to kill over.

BANG BANG BANG.

Suddenly the horses whinnied and reared up. The driver shouted louder, attempting to control them.

"We might be overturned," Jane announced as she felt the carriage rock. She stood up, hunched over, reaching again for the door.

This time, TallMan did not stop Jane.

Jane pushed open the door to see what was causing the rocking of the carriage. She was able to see one horse had broken free and was galloping away. Eliza followed Jane and hopped out of the rocking carriage.

The driver noted the other horse was agitated and also tugging on his restraints. Now the driver hopped down from his perch and got on the last horse to untangle it and soothe it. As soon as the horse was a bit calmer, the driver worked to untangle the leather straps.

Eunice and TallMan now both got down from the carriage to see if they might also aid in some way.

As the last strap was loosened and the driver was about to dismount, the driver waved off the approaching TallMan with, "I've got him under control, thank you, Sir."

TallMan stepped back and then the horse, with the driver still mounted on the steed's back, yanked away from all restraints.

The force of the pull caused the carriage to now tip over and precariously balance onto two of the four wheels.

Instinctively, TallMan stood as barrier between the bucking horse and the ladies. BANG again.

Then, as the driver was shouting at the horse with, "Easy. Whoa. Be calm. Whoa..."

The horse gave a vicious kick against the carriage, yanked away from all the leather restraints tying the animal to the vehicle, and galloped away with the surprised driver clinging to his back.

The party could hear their driver yelling, "...Stop...Please...Whoa...Whoooa aaa..." fading into the distance.

Jane, speechless, looked at the debris of the carriage. It had fallen flat on its side... four wheels still spinning in the air. One wheel had broken to bits.

"I do not profess a knowledge of engineering," Eliza explained, "...but I would say even if we could manage to tip this thing back up onto the wheels and find a horse... we cannot move forward with three out of the four wheels."

"No," TallMan said with practical efficiency, "but we can use the broken wheel for firewood."

"Firewood?" Jane asked askance, "Are you implying we should set up a fire and remain here? What of the villains who shot at us? Would it not be better to walk back?"

"We have come quite a distance, Jane," Eunice started, "It would take us perhaps two days to march back by foot... We do not have food, and... there is luggage to carry..."

"And I estimate we are half way to Meeting Town," TallMan added, "So, in either direction it will take time. Best if we start out in the morning."

As the last sounds of whinnying horses and the shouting driver faded, and as the dust from the upset carriage settled, the small group became aware of the laughter of young boys.

Eunice spoke softly, "I believe we have been attacked by bored youths who have found some gunpowder and firearms."

"To what end?" Jane asked, "Will they attack and take our merger goods?"

TallMan replied, "I do not think we are in danger. Our destruction was meant for their amusement. I believe they have achieved their goal, which was to scare away the horses with loud sounds."

Eunice added, "Listen. Silence. They have gone. Their entire purpose was to scare the horses and then leave before they are held accountable for their misdeeds. Still silence... I do not believe they will return."

"So," Jane remarked, "We are the victims of mischief for the sake of mischief and nothing more? Do they not care how they have greatly inconvenienced us, and damaged a carriage, and possibly endangered the life of the driver?"

"I do not expect our driver will return..." Eunice added, "He will need to get both horses. Find a stable for the night. Then return to his employer as quickly as possible lest he lose his job. He will not take the time to return and retrieve us."

Eliza Lucas added, with a tone of anger and foreboding, "We are alone. It will be dark soon. Too far to walk back, but uncertain how far from our destination. Unable to meet Susanna Wright. Unprepared to spend the night in this... wilderness...Why we must have travelled 40 miles by now."

"Is there anything we can do to get to safety?" Jane asked.

3 CHAPTER 90: (JUNE 1776) The Flickering Light of a Candle Outside the Barn

With a dramatic flourish. Henry Mossop, the Irish opera singer who had recently proclaimed doom upon the attendees at the secret barn meeting, lit the flame of the candle. He slipped a fat cigar between his lips and lowered his face to the candle flame as he sucked in, causing the tip of the rolled tobacco leaves to glow. Calmly, he exhaled a billowing cloud of smoke into the face of his nearby indebted henchman. Mr. Mossop liked to show disdain for those in his employ with small gestures of disregard. He especially liked to abuse the ones who were desperately dependent upon him for money.

While waving the smoke away, one man coughed and said to Henry Mossop, "I thought you stated you wouldn't smoke because of your voice."

While guarding the candle flame from the evening gusts of wind, the opera singer retorted, "My singing career is dead. Audiences don't fancy the aria da capo as much as they had in the past. The orchestras are growing larger to ghastly and vulgar proportions... I need to look to other retirement options. I believe I have found one which is quite lucrative."

Henry Mossop looked at the light flickering in the wind, hoping it would not blow out.

"But," the second man protested, "Opera is popular entertainment... I mean, the story lines can be discouraging, but they do leave one with a lesson to ponder, do they not?"

Henry Mossop fumed, "Why do you think I've allied with Lady Sarah Wilson, that deceitful woman? She knows how to contrive gold from the pockets of men better than any performer."

"She does leave a man with the impression that he can do no wrong..." the first man replied.

Henry Mossop took a deep breath as he puffed, making the tip of his cigar tobacco glow, as he snarled,

"*Christoph Willibald Gluck*. I hate him. He is forcing new innovations upon the audience, which make me recede to the back of the stage. If I continued to work with Mr. Gluck, no longer would I be granted permission to shine as the vocal virtuoso I was destined to be."

29

While waiting for a response to the candle flame signal, the other man reasoned, "But Christoph Gluck simply proposes one philosophy when he creates an opera. Surely, there are others who develop operas."

"Mr. Gluck," Henry Mossop spat as he knocked ash off the end of his cigar, "has abolished the *secco*."

"I don't know what that means..." The second man commented.

Annoyed, Henry Mossop snapped, "Abolishing the *secco* means one cannot discern between an aria and recitative. He is adding drama and dance like a French street performer. The chorus is so loud they drown me out. Who needs twenty-four violins? What was wrong with... I don't know... ten? And, why can I no longer exit with my own aria?"

The first man replied, "An opera is more than song... there is a story which captivates the audience…"

Henry Mossop, the former *primo uomo*, choked with emotion as he responded, "Story? There is no story. The sub-plots which add texture to the theme… gone. Completely removed. Baroque opera is dead. *Jommelli* and *Verazi* are producing nonsense… utter rubbish!" His voice trailed off into a brooding mutter, "I see the royals get wealthy with no regard to morality, and it is about time I profit, as well, by the same practices."

The second man, not hearing Henry Mossop's final vow to abandon all morality in his pursuit of wealth, responded to Mr. Mossop's first statement, saying, "You mean Opera Seria… melodrama serio… will no longer be the entertainment of European nobles?" The second man gasped in disbelief as he tried to comprehend this change, adding, "Was not Alcyone by Marin Marais so popular in Versailles it has been performed for nearly 70 years? The sinking ship scene is so dramatic!"

The first man added with a light laugh, "In Dublin, they still speak of how you, Mr. Mossop, faced off Thomas Barry by scheduling Othello to play on the same day Mr. Barry's Othello had been advertised for three weeks prior at the Theater Royal back in 1762."

"Mr. Barry deserved it," Henry Mossop defended as he guarded the flame of the candle while the cigar dangled out of the corner of his mouth.

"Indeed," The first man replied.

Henry Mossop continued, "I had to use the Eaton Orphans as an excuse to book the same night Mr. Barry did. The nerve to reschedule his Othello the next night, as if he could spy on my show and improve on my performance!"

"But you got the attention you wanted, Mr. Mossop," The second man added.

Now feeling smug, Henry Mossop advised, "What you need to learn is to really accuse the innocent. That is why I also asked Sheriff Booker to arrest Thomas Barry and fine him five hundred pounds! I won in running him out of town at the end of the season in 1766."

"Wasn't that 1767?"The first man asked.

Henry Mossop, faded *primo uomo* opera singer spat, "The season can fall over the new year, imbecile!"

"Is that when," the second man asked, "you took over both theaters and a few years later found you didn't have enough money to keep 'em both operating, Mr. Mossop?" The man stepped back into the shadows as he continued, "Ironic, that if you had cooperated with Mr. Barry, you could have offered more variety and increased the sale of tickets, but since you drove him out of town, you couldn't manage both theaters and so... lost both of them..." he mused.

Anger whipped up inside Henry Mossop like a roaring lion. He said firmly, "I did not lose both theaters! I gave up the stage on Crow street and did not know Dawson was opening up an abandoned theater on Capel street! I had to endure atrocities."

"Such as?" the second man prodded.

Mossop replied, "Such as a public scene that actress Mrs. Burden made. She demanded I pay her the five pounds a week I owed her... as if her acting warranted such a royal amount."

"So ticket sales didn't allow you to pay your actors?" the first man asked, "Some say the choices a man made in the past will be the ones he makes in the future. Will you pay us?"

Defensive, *primo uomo* Henry Mossop replied, "I got into debt because I have exquisite tastes. I didn't declare bankruptcy until 1772 and it could have happened to anybody. Luckily, I met Lady Sarah Wilson and she invited me over here and we have started a much more profitable enterprise..."

The second man stepped to the first man and whispered, "He's not going to answer you. But if we leave now, neither of us will get paid... better to risk it and complete the task..."

The first man nodded in agreement to the second man.

"What are you two whispering about?" Henry Mossop demanded.

The first man replied with, "The profitable enterprise you developed with Sarah Wilson. That is a situation which would be jeopardized by these very meetings at this here barn, would it not? Mr. Mossop? Thomas Barry's actions impacted your opera ticket sales back in Ireland. Would not these barn meetings likewise threaten your business you created with Sarah Wilson?"

"This is why I have developed the signal," Henry Mossop retorted, pointing to the flickering flame of the candle.

"But," the second man shrugged, "They are still meeting inside that barn. Your candle is not doing anything."

Henry Mossop, ignoring the babblings of his mutinous sycophants, extracted a bit of colored glass from his pocket and held it over the flame of the candle to create a multi-colored glow. Then, Henry Mossop blew the candle flame out.

"The signal is now complete," Henry Mossop replied. "Hurry. We have not much time before it starts."

"Before what starts?" The second man asked, "You've been secretive about what this signal will do..."

"I pay you to follow orders, not to question me," Henry Mossop barked as he moved away.

"If we get paid..." The first man muttered, but reluctantly followed Henry Mossop.

A moment later, the deliberating

second man also grudgingly followed Henry Mossop and the first man. Quietly, all three melted into the shadows of the fields and without a word, headed to the perimeter of the farm.

The gentle windy rustle in the air was punctuated by the lull of a cacophony of animal noises: soft grunts of steeds, the bleating of sheep, the occasional clang of a bell around a cow's neck peppered by the oink of a pig.

The light from a glowing lantern inside the barn streamed beams from between wooden planks making up the barn walls. Silence had begun to fall overall.

The stable boys had finished walking the horses to cool them down, and finally brushed them. They were now ready to enter the barn and put the horses back into their stalls. They approached the barn door just as the occupants inside were opening it. The meeting attendees were ready to vacate for the night and return home to their families and dinner. Then, a loud shout was heard.

4 CHAPTER 91: (JUNE 1776) The Horses Retreat

Henry Mossop and his two men had already melted into the shadows after having lit a candle, covering the flame with colored glass, and promptly leaving the fields before the action started.

The stable boys had returned and prepared the horses to enter to the barn. Just then, the meeting's occupants opened the door, about to disband for the night... but a shout was heard.

It echoed across the valley.

Unaccustomed to this, the stable boys froze with rope leads in their hands. They did not know if they should flee with the horses or continue to lead them to their stalls.

Likewise, the meeting attendees also heard the noise and did not know what to make of it. The eldest stable boy quickly mounted one of the horses he was leading and kept hold of the ropes of the other horses and shouted at the others, "They're here. Quick. Follow me!"

The other boys, scrambled to mount their horses. One boy, smaller than the others, did not have time to fully mount and was barely able to push himself up so his belly was over the back of the steed before his horse followed the others. It was a rocky scramble as the boy clung to the mane of the horse as he tried to get into a straddle position while it was now running. This boy lost the leads of the other horses he held, but the remaining steeds kept pace following the rest of the troupe. Back over the horizon they fled.

The meeting occupants were uncertain why the stable boys took off. They found it rather peculiar. The air now became still.

No wind.

No animal noises... just the retreating huffs and hoof stomps of the horses pounding away far over the hillside.

The meeting's occupants started to discuss this odd phenomenon. Abruptly, red coated soldiers, the kings men, appeared from nowhere and raced down on the barn like grain funneling along a silo.

A meeting attendee who had stood gazing at the retreating shadowy horses, turned and peered across the field in the opposite direction. There he saw the flood of the Kings Men descending upon the barn.

This meeting attendee shouted a warning giving the other occupants only a few seconds to react.

5 CHAPTER 92: (JUNE 1776) Bryce Dashes From the Dunlap Home

Bryce Aiden Tyler realized he did not have enough time to continue this conversation with Mrs. Dunlap, the Printer, and Polly, whom the presumed widow Jane Hargreaves had rescued from the roadside.

Bryce, former business partner to Jane's deceased Uncle Floyd, needed to discover why Jane had just left the mansion of Lady Sarah Wilson. Bryce had convinced Magistrate Karl Pinkney to accompany him on this quest and the magistrate was waiting in the carriage outside the Dunlap home.

"Mrs. Dunlap," Bryce stated as he stood up in the Dunlap living room while pushing back the empty tea cup on the table, "I thank you for the offer of libation, but my priority is to find Jane. Please pardon my brusque departure."

"Naturally," Mrs. Dunlap smiled as she rose to her feet. "I understand you are concerned for Jane. She is a lovely friend."

"I'm worried, as well, Mr. Tyler," Polly stated. "Jane, and her driver, and her Lady's maid were... well, I owe them my life... and the life of my soon to be born." Polly looked down at her pregnant abdomen, then looked up at Bryce Aiden Tyler and continued, "Please let me know if I can be of help to you in any way."

"It does not surprise me," Bryce started, "to know that Miss Hargreaves has fostered loyalty, friendship and comfort in you, her new friends. In my short acquaintance with her, I have found Miss Hargreaves to be tenacious when it comes to doing the right thing... even at her own peril. Please excuse me."

Bryce shouted over his shoulder, "I can see myself out. No need to trouble your butler. Thank you."

Polly called after him as she struggled to stand to an unstable position, "I think, Mr. Tyler, that if Jane is that determined, she may have gone to the Meeting Town by herself to investigate the situation we spoke of..."

Then, the front door slammed shut.

"Jane... she..." Polly, tears filling her eyes, looked to Mrs. Dunlap.

"Now, now. Dear. I'm sure Jane is fine..." Mrs. Dunlap comforted, "That Bryce Aiden Tyler fellow will find her. He strikes me as quite determined..."

"Mrs. Dunlap," Polly explained as she gripped the hands of Mrs. Dunlap, "Jane rescued me and my unborn child. She paid for my lodgings here with that boar meat made into Silversmith's bacoun. She told me she would complete her Uncle Floyd's mission and make sure I would never again live in fear of another Indian slave raid by asking Benjamin Franklin to write a letter to the King of England requesting cessation of all Colonial slave trading. She risked herself for me, a wretch of an Irish lass. She befriended me, an act which would bring her shame in her own social circles."

Mrs. Dunlap soothed, "Now, now... don't become agitated, Polly,"

"What if something terrible were to befall Jane? It would be my fault." Polly sank into a chair, her skirts filling with air from her rapid descent. The soft pillows of fabric slowly deflated as Polly's palms covered her eyes to squeeze out the guilt she felt.

"It is never fair," Mrs. Dunlap patted

Polly on her back, "when honorable intentions incite the jealous anger of evil-doers, who seem bent on snuffing out good."

"Snuff out?" Polly exclaimed as she locked eyes with Mrs. Dunlap, "I pray, Mrs. Dunlap, answer me this: Do you know something about Jane's disappearance that you did... not ... share with me or that Bryce Aiden Tyler?"

6 CHAPTER 93: (JUNE 1776) The Carriage Got Out Just In Time

Just as the barn meeting attendees saw the stable boys retreat with the horses, and heard their fellow meeting attendant shout a warning that the King's soldiers were descending upon them, they scrambled.

Safely inside the carriage and out of the way of the raid, Peter Timothy, Silversmith, Jane's Lady's Maid, and Jane's hired driver, Billy Dawes looked back. The carriage had just returned a baby lamb, Peter Timothy temporarily named, "snowflake" to the neighbor's fields. This was the alpaca lamb, which Henry Mossop's men wanted to slaughter for their dinner.

Far away, up along the road, the three heard the noise of the militia's raid although they were a great distance away. They heard the sound of advancing soldier's drums. It was dark now and the three could not discern who was attacking whom.

Billy Dawes yanked on his reins halting the horses. He leapt off his perch. Once his feet thudded on the dirt road, he raced to open the carriage door.

"Do you hear that?" Billy Dawes whispered hoarsely.

Peter Timothy answered, "Sounds like an organized raid."

Silversmith whispered, "I suppose that is why Henry Mossop lit that candle to signal the raid."

Peter Timothy listened, then said, "It sounds as if it could be the Red Coats."

Billy Dawes asked, "Do we stay? Do we return to the barn to rescue some? Do we continue on our original course to town?"

Peter Timothy replied, " I do not think we need to risk being arrested by the Red Coats."

Silversmith added, "I agree, Billy. Let's get to the Inn. We don't have a plan to rescue the others, so could very well get arrested ourselves. Plus, we summoned Miss Jane. We need to meet her at the Inn and report what we have discovered."

With a nod, Billy Dawes silently pushed the door shut. He untethered the horses and jumped back up onto his perch.

Inside the carriage, Silversmith looked at Peter Timothy and whispered, "You rescued me just in time."

With a snap, Billy Dawes hurried the horses onward. Wooden wheels bumped against rocks and dips in the road creating a very bumpy ride.

"Miss Silversmith, you overheard information. Mr. Dawes created the plan to extract you from an awkward situation. I simply feigned ownership of a lamb to prevent it from becoming somebody's dinner and provide a distraction so you could enter the carriage unnoticed. But neither Mr. Dawes nor I anticipated an organized raid of Red Coats on the barn meeting..."

With a cold wind in his face, Billy glanced backward over his shoulder. He could no longer see the barn, but he could still hear the shouts and cries punctuated by the blast from ignited gunpowder. Billy Dawes anxiously snapped his reins to speed the galloping horses even faster.

Silversmith clung to the bench on which she was sitting and said to Mr. Timothy, "I appreciate Mr. Dawes' tenacity and expert strategy. You both did extract me from a perilous situation. I believe Henry Mossop could do away with me and feel no guilt. Billy Dawes, by contrast is a good... a... good friend to have, don't you think?"

The carriage wheel hit a large rock, causing the carriage to shift and the horses to whinny, but Billy Dawes regained control and kept urging the horses to continue the pace.

Peter Timothy, relieved the carriage was still moving forward, replied to Silversmith, "Mr. Dawes is a very good ally. An expert driver. He cares very much for you, Silversmith." Peter took a breath, then asked, "Your mistress... Jane Hargreaves, is it? When is she expected to arrive?"

7 CHAPTER 94: (JUNE 1776) The King's Men Descend. Susanna grabs Button

As the carriage sped forward toward the town inn; As Henry Mossop and his men faded into the shadows; As the stable boys escaped with all the horses but moments before the King's Men descended onto the barn, the barn meeting attendees scrambled.

Button looked at the Farmer, who quickly abandoned his precious water jugs and ran out the back door, following four others as they faded into the darkness outside. The farmer did not even look back to see if Button was with him. It was as if the Farmer had made an agreement with these other four people and they escaped together.

Button helplessly froze as he realized he had just spoken boldly in front of this group of strangers.

He had just informed the Farmer that he would no longer help serve water at these secret meetings and would put the disturbing memories of the loss of his wife, Polly, behind him as he was determined to embrace the next chapter of his life.

But, now, everybody was screaming and running around where Button stood frozen. He did not know what to do. Benjamin Franklin ran up to Button and physically pushed him toward Miss Susanna Wright.

Mr. Franklin shouted to be heard above the panicky noise, "Go with her. Now!"

Before Button could react, he felt Susanna Wright grab his arm and tug him. He trailed behind her bewildered as if he were a running toddler's blanket being dragged along the floor.

Susanna Wright, Quaker woman, led Button to the back corner of the barn, behind a pile of hay.

She grabbed what appeared to be the handle of a common pitchfork, and yanked it. Part of the hay seemed to sift down a hole in the floor.

Susanna Wright had opened a trap door.

Deftly, she hopped down a ladder, as if she had taken this route several times before. "Quickly Button, before they enter the barn!" she ordered.

Without a word, Button obeyed.

He dropped down the short ladder and landed hard on dusty ground.

In the darkness, Susanna waited to hear the thud of Button's feet hitting the floor, then she pulled a rope, which closed the door.

The motion of it also shook some hay on top of the trap door in the floor of the barn, hiding it again, just before the red coats entered the barn.

"I thought you were a Quaker," Button whispered perplexed.

"One's religion," Susanna whispered back, "is not a measure as to how much knowledge one can amass and employ in emergency situations. Please be quiet and follow me."

Susanna picked up her skirts with one hand and placed a hand on Button's mouth to indicate how imperative it was to remain silent.

He nodded that he understood.

In the darkness, Susanna Wright took his hand and placed it firmly on the wall.

She clutched the hem of her skirts with one hand and placed her free hand along the side of the small tunnel they were moving through, sliding her palm along to guide her.

The only sound Button heard was the rustle of her skirts right ahead of him.

Then, Button heard the clomping of leather boots above him and ensuing shouts of the attendees resisting arrest and protesting the orders issued by these Lobster Backs.

As Susanna and Button continued along the dirt tunnel, the sound of the soldiers' ruckus above them had faded.

Then, Button tripped in the darkness.

Susanna cautioned with a sharp whisper, "Stay close. Stay hunched over or you will hit your head. Keep your palm on the wall or else you'll get disoriented. Follow my directions and you will live."

Then there was silence... above... had the Red Coats, the King's Men, arrested all the attendees?

"Do not trip, again," Susanna warned as she remained hunched down to accommodate the tiny dirt corridor.

"But the Farmer... who brought me..." Button protested, "Should we not return to make sure he is safe?"

Susanna replied with a whisper, "We cannot go back. Although you may not see him again for a very long while. Farmer had made arrangements. He is safe. The King's Men will patrol around the barn for a few more hours. Forward is our only option."

Button, scraping his hand along the dirt tunnel wall, asked with curiosity, "Why did others not escape down this tunnel? Why only us two?"

Still moving forward, Susanna reluctantly replied, "We all have different escape paths planned before we go to any meeting site. We cannot all escape the same way or we might all be caught by His Majesty's crimson oafs."

"Why did you take me along?" Button asked.

"Because," Susanna replied as she gingerly stepped forward, sliding her hand along the dirt walls, "you were bold enough to speak your mind on freedom… but as a newcomer. I assumed you did not have an escape plan. Farmer told me he had a plan, but confessed there was no room for you in that plan. None of us really thought there would be a raid, but we all verified our escapes before we met. Was I correct in my assumption, Mr. water fetcher?"

"I feel as if I am constantly escaping from something…" Button bemoaned as his back started to ache from the hunched over position he maintained.

Susanna replied with a whisper over her shoulder, "Well, that is only because the King feels he runs this land even though he did nothing to establish it." Susanna sighed, "We all feel as if we are constantly running without making any progress! Yet we must continue to move... regardless of our feelings..." She reminded him as she quickened her pace.

"I am a man of no import," Button stated

Susanna stopped, turned around, and without being able to see him, Button felt her finger jab into his shoulder.

Susanna said quietly, "I speak English, French, Italian and can read Latin. I have been educated in England, but I can be practical, as well. Years ago, my father, brother and I started a ferry across the Susquehanna River with two dug-out canoes to transport both cattle and people. I can get people moved to where they need to be... much as I am doing with you. I can recognize an educated man even if he is in rags,

Button, thou fetcher of water. I can tell you possess sufficient intelligence to do more than refill our drinking vessels during a meeting. The words you spoke betray your intellect."

Susanna turned around, and pressed her dirty hand to the side of the wall to guide her along as she continued to move forward.

Realizing Susanna was getting too far ahead of him, Button quickened his pace to keep up. "And?" Button prodded.

Susanna kept up her quickened pace as she replied over her shoulder.

Susanna Wright said, "So, doubtless, that Henry Mossop fellow, that Opera singing *primo uomo*, gave some sort of signal after he vacated our meeting for the raid. He must be getting gold from the king or some valuable incentive."

Button asked, "But wasn't he one of the attendees at the barn meeting? Even if he did not believe in the topic, why would he betray so many innocent people who are just trying to understand how to live in this land?"

"I suspect," Susanna Wright started, "Although I have no proof..."

"Proof of what?" Button asked.

Susanna Wright sighed and, without looking back, she continued, "I suspect that Henry Mossop is somehow involved in selling Colonial slaves. I even had my suspicions when I saw how he looked at you and took such a great dislike to you... that..."

Susanna fell silent unsure if she should speak her mind.

"Please go on," Button prodded.

"Button," Susanna stated, "You told everybody that you had escaped captivity."

"Yes. What of it?" Button asked.

"Have you not considered," Susanna Wright continued, "That the reason Henry Mossop dealt you such a thrashing as he exited the barn, was because Mr. Mossop was the one who hired those Indians to raid your cabin and you had just announced to him that you are his profitable inventory gone missing. He may even be the one who called the raid."

"You mean, I have unwittingly endangered the lives of all the people in that meeting because I announced I had escaped?" Button did not know how to comprehend this information.

Susanna took a breath and then she stopped at a certain spot.

Both of her hands were now feeling the side of the wall as if she was looking for something. "Never you mind. Mr. Mossop may have sufficient gold to hire others to raid your cabin, but I am relying on the fact he does not wish to spend more trying to find you again... Although, you are the only one who can provide us details which may help in preventing future raids...but I would assume he would rather sell the victims he already has... Well, to be safe, we shall hide you for the nonce.."

"How long is a 'nonce'?" Button asked.

"I would advise," Susanna started as she found a knot of rope sticking out of a small hole in the dirt wall, "that you make staying alive and freedom your priority. Should you be seen in public, one of Mossop's men may identify you, and you risk getting re-captured and shipped off to a foreign land to be sold as a slave, assuming you survive the journey...."

Susanna tugged the rope.

"I will follow your lead, then... for the nonce." Button conceded. A small hatch opened up in the wall.

Susanna wright knelt down on her hands and knees.

She crawled through an inclined tunnel leading to the surface. She knocked on the ceiling in a rhythmic pattern.

A moment later, the opening was revealed. All Button saw was the brief shadow of a man and he heard a grunt as the man heaved the heavy barrier aside.

Susanna then emerged in an alleyway behind a wall lined with barrels and debris. Nearby shops and merchant carts were in the process of closing up for the night. Pedestrians clutched their cloaks about them to shield them from the winds.

Some held lit lanterns as they walked along the street.

Susanna Wright looked around as she slapped her hands together to get the dust off her palms, then shook out her skirts. She looked down at Button, indicating it was safe for him to emerge.

The smell of horses frequenting the streets became intense. The clomping and conversation of people now filled Button's ears. Susanna Wright impatiently waited for button to emerge. The man, who had opened the passageway door, closed it after Button surfaced, and went back to minding his street cart, packing it up for the night, along with the other vendors nearby.

This cart vendor treated Susanna and Button as if they were customers.

He was no common vendor, but a posted lookout, Susanna quietly explained to Button.

Button wondered how many lookouts were minding escape paths for the people who were meeting and expecting a raid from the King's men. How many people were secretly harboring a desire for independence and freedom, yet unable to voice it publicly?

A soldier clad in a red jacket walked up to the cart. He seemed interested in the wares of the vendor. Susanna immediately picked up an object on the cart, examining it carefully as if she were considering buying it.

The vendor turned to the Red Coated soldier and mentioned, "I'll be just a moment, Sir." He turned to Susanna wright and wrapped the object in paper, tying it with twine.

He handed the bundle to Button, as if Button were Susanna's servant.

The cart vendor addressed Susanna and said, "Please come and see us again, Madame". Then he turned to Button and shook a warning finger, "Now don't drop it or your mistress will be very upset. It was my last one."

"Thank you," Susanna replied simply and started to walk away.

The cart vendor smiled at Susanna, turned his back on her and Button and approached the Red coated soldier, addressing him with solicitous obsequious fawning, "And how sir, may we serve you today? Could I interest you in...." The soldier was intrigued by the wares in the cart.

Susanna and Button quickly walked away seeking the privacy of a small alley between two buildings

Once out of earshot, Button whispered to Susanna, making sure to keep his eyes downcast, "Earlier you mentioned I may be viewed as lost profits. Are you saying the redcoats would arrest me because I spoke as I wanted to at a private meeting after escaping an attack on my own home?" Button asked, "Why would I not be allowed to speak freely?"

Susanna Wright, walking rapidly, glanced left then right. She motioned Button to follow her quickly down the street. In silence, they hurried along until she stopped in front of a storage hut. Susanna opened the door, walked in, then walked out again and glanced left and right to ensure the street was vacant. She then motioned for Button to follow her inside the hut. She closed the door behind them both.

She leaned into Button and clearly, firmly, yet quietly stated, "The King still believes this country belongs to him and he can treat the occupants any way he pleases."

Her eyes darted briefly to confirm nobody else could hear her before she continued, "If you want the freedom to speak... or the freedom to live in the home you built with your wife on property you owned... then help us convince His Majesty. I saved you once, yet I cannot guarantee safety in this current environment. The environment needs to change. The way to change an environment peaceably is to draft a document in secret. "

"You mean, finish a letter to the king asking him to leave our colonies unfettered?" Button asked.

Susanna replied, "Button, what are you prepared to risk? How much does freedom mean to you? You may never discover what happened to your wife, but you can do something to ensure that slave raids for profit do not happen again to peaceful Colonists. What are you prepared to do?"

8 CHAPTER 95: (JUNE 1776)
Magistrate Changes Directions

In the back of the Magistrate's carriage, Bryce Aiden Tyler discussed the situation.

"You see, Magistrate Pinkney, Lady Sarah Wilson's slaves didn't know where Jane had gone. Mrs. Dunlap thought Jane had gone shopping... without her hired driver, Billy Dawes. However, as I was leaving their home to return to your carriage, I overheard a new friend of Miss

Hargreaves... a woman called Polly... who said Jane may have gone ahead to this place they call the Meeting Town."

Karl Pinkney, Magistrate, replied, "Oh, yes. I know of it. It is not the official name, of course, but 'tis rumored all the Firebrands meet there to try and rebel against His Majesty's rule of the Colonies."

"Magistrate Pinkney," Bryce Aiden Tyler carefully chose his words, "I am concerned the life of a woman is at stake. Could I have your word that regardless of whatever political sides we encounter, that we set that aside and deal solely with the lives at hand?"

As the carriage rolled along, Magistrate Karl Pinkney thought. He thumped on the roof of the carriage. A moment later, the carriage halted and a red-coated driver opened the door with a, "Yes, sir?"

Magistrate Karl Pinkney said, "Change directions. Take the road to Meeting Town... and take the path which the hired carriages oft times take."

The red-coated soldier nodded in affirmation and closed the door, then turned the carriage around taking a different route.

Magistrate Pinkney explained to Bryce Aiden Tyler, "Miss Hargreaves did not have her driver with her, so if she went, she would had to have hired a carriage, I suspect."

"I thank you, Magistrate," Bryce said sincerely, "I do hope your suspicions are correct".

9 CHAPTER 96: (JUNE 1776) Polly Translates

"Polly! Polly!" Mrs. Dunlap shouted as she burst into her living room, startling Polly, who was quietly reading.

"Mrs. Dunlap!" Polly exclaimed.

"I just got the rest of it!" Excitedly, Mrs. Dunlap's heart raced as she held high above her head, a letter. She stopped, clutching the crumpled letter to her heart, as she looked up to the heavens with a relieved sigh, "Finally!"

Polly threw her book down on the little table and struggled to stand up. "The rest of Mr. Livingston's thoughts on that letter to His Majesty?"

Simple tasks, such as walking, were more akin to waddling. but standing up from a soft overstuffed sofa, was nearly impossible. Her pregnant belly made Polly long for the days when she didn't have to plan each movement with precision strategy.

Nodding her head with impatience, Mrs. Dunlap reached down and yanked Polly's arm, nearly separating Polly's feet from the floor. As Polly gingerly stood on her own, she smiled and peered at the letter in Mrs. Dunlap's hand.

"Indeed it is! Now! We must get it translated quickly! We must get it distributed as soon as possible." Polly smiled. "Mrs. Dunlap. I must apologize to you."

"Whatever for, child?" Mrs. Dunlap asked.

"I was so concerned about Jane's disappearance, I accused you of concealing information from that nice gentleman, Mr. Tyler. "

"Oh! Do you think I, of all people, would conceal anything that titillating if I did indeed know it? You are silly, my girl. Quite silly indeed." Mrs. Dunlap laughed, "I don't know anything about Jane's current predicament, but I am certain she is simply shopping... Let us not be distracted, Polly." Mrs. Dunlap shook the letter in the air, "German translating, eh?"

Polly waddled straight over to the bookshelf and withdrew a book. She tapped the German to English dictionary, pulling it off the shelf.

With a grand exaggerated gesture and a short curtsy, Mrs. Dunlap giggled as she handed the letter over to Polly.

Polly immediately situated herself at the writing desk, smoothing out the letter. Polly looked at the blank vellum still scrolled up with the ribbon around it.

She smiled.

Polly pulled open a drawer and extracted the pages where she had penned the first few sentences from Mr. Robert Livingston's previous letter and set those to one side. She slid the inkwell and quill closer to her.

"If Mr. Livingston completed his thoughts, I can finish my draft and then transfer it to Button's Vellum to ensure the meaning of the words will last a long time."

Mrs. Dunlap brought over a lit candle for Polly to see by. "Penning your final version onto your husband's vellum is the perfect way to remember him, Polly. You'll be able to proudly tell your child that his father did participate in the Unification of the Colonies."

The candle flickered brightly. It was going to be a very long night, indeed.

Mrs. Dunlap added, "And what do you think of this, Polly?" Mrs. Dunlap inhaled, "After the English version is signed by the Continental Congress, I can ask my husband..."

"The famous printer, John Dunlap?" Polly smiled

Mrs. Dunlap giggled, "Yes. Mr. Dunlap will give your translation to his German newspaper friend, Mr. Henrich Miller, to let all his readers know that the united colonies are now free and independent states."

"Do you think, Mrs. Dunlap," Polly mused, "That the Continental Congress would not only sign it, but that the King of England would really agree to it? Peacefully?"

10 CHAPTER 97: (JUNE 1776) Magistrate & Bryce Follow Hunch to Meeting Town

As Magistrate Karl Pinkney and Bryce Aiden Tyler changed course to head to Meeting Town, both Bryce and Magistrate Pinkney reviewed what they knew of Jane Hargreaves' disappearance from the estate of Lady Sarah Wilson.

"Mr. Tyler..." Magistrate Karl Pinkney started.

"Oh, please refer to me as Bryce as I consider you a friend now for helping me find Jane Hargreaves before anything untoward happens to her."

The Magistrate cleared his throat, "Indeed. Bryce, I would..." Bryce interrupted him, "And how may I refer to you?"

The Magistrate, abruptly becoming perturbed at these interruptions, sharply replied, "Magistrate Pinkney, as you have done."

Bryce smiled and nodded.

As his carriage bumped along the road, the Magistrate leaned in toward Bryce Aiden Tyler, former business partner to the deceased Floyd Hargreaves, whose body the Magistrate and his brother had collected a while ago.

The Magistrate looked Bryce in his eyes and said plainly, "We have been given no proof that your Miss Hargreaves has gone to this Meeting Town. The only reason we are heading in this direction is because you overheard a woman call out to you that she suspected your Jane Hargreaves may have gone there... it is not what we would call conclusive proof."

"I realize the odds are not in our favor, but I do appreciate your assistance very much," Bryce Aiden Tyler affirmed.

"Then," The magistrate leaned against a down filled square cushion. "Perhaps you can inform me of other threads of information you have overheard so that we may assemble a full tapestry of your Miss Hargreaves."

He took a breath before he cautiously continued, "For instance, how did you conclude we should investigate this Lady Sarah Wilson's estate?"

Bryce Aiden Tyler nodded as he explained, "Floyd Hargreaves' devoted butler, whom you have already met..."

The magistrate interrupted him, "Yes. Witherspoon. I do recall."

Bryce continued, "Indeed. Witherspoon received a letter from Silversmith which explained that Miss Hargreaves administered a test of sorts to her tailor friend."

"Oh, I recall," Magistrate Karl Pinkney looked up as he recollected. "Mr. Tweedbottom was there when my brother and I and the doctor collected the body of Floyd Hargreaves."

"Yes. That's the fellow," Bryce affirmed.

"What sort of test would your Jane Hargreaves have given this tailor Tweedbottom?"

Bryce explained, "Although Miss Hargreaves was not aware that Mr. Tweedbottom was also invited to the estate of Lady Sarah Wilson, Mr. Tweedbottom unexpectedly showed up, yet he was not there to console Jane... I mean, Miss Hargreaves, as she expected."

"Go on," The magistrate prodded.

"So," Bryce continued, "she wrote a poem for Mr. Tweedbottom and handed it to him. She observed if Mr. Tweedbottom required his odd Voigtländer."

"His what?" The magistrate's brow furrowed.

"Eye ring." Bryce explained.

"Why on earth would one draw a ring around one's eye?" the magistrate asked shrugging.

"The Hargreaves family," Bryce Aiden Tyler clarified, "has a propensity to invent things."

"Invent?" The magistrate incredulously challenged.

"Indeed," Bryce defended, "As a result of their curiosity and dexterity..."

The magistrate interrupted scoffing, "which became all those so called inventions?"

"Yes," Bryce affirmed, "which means the Hargreaves are also attracted to individuals who procure new gadgets. I believe this eye ring was the foundation of the friendship between Miss Hargreaves and Mr. Tweedbottom. The eye ring was a new device to discuss."

Shaking his hand, palm forward, the Magistrate stopped Bryce from speaking and said, "Your explanation does not enlighten me as to what a Voit...Vog...that... lander...this eye ring of which you speak... I do not know what it is... I must understand what it is if Miss Hargreaves considered it important in her test."

Bryce nodded, now understanding, and explained, "Johann Friedrich Voigtländer is an Austrian fellow who studied optometry in London and developed this device... a lens for use in only one eye."

"How peculiar," The magistrate scoffed, "To chop spectacles in half and consider that an invention..."

Bryce continued, "Some call it a monocle."

The magistrate retorted, "Some may call it preposterous. It will never sell in a store. Impractical. But, you stray from our topic, Mr. Tyler... Bryce. What of this Tweedbottom fellow?"

Bryce added, "Mr. Tweedbottom owns this monocle device, but I do not believe it is available to be purchased. It is a unique object which can be used to start a conversation."

"And what," Magistrate Pinkney asked, "is the inductive conclusion as to why this monocle owned by that tailor, Mr. Tweedbottom, is important? You have, after all, come to some conclusion by eliminating all other possibilities, have you not?"

"Miss Hargreaves tested Mr. Tweedbottom to see if he can only read with his eye ring. He did." Bryce explained.

The magistrate waved away the explanation with, "So, the fellow has poor eyesight. What of it? With printed matter becoming more popular, I would expect magnification devices would also increase in popularity."

"I suspect," Bryce clarified, "that a lens, such as the one used in an eye ring... or a monocle... was used in the murder of Floyd Hargreaves."

"Or," the magistrate leaned his head back against the wall of the bouncing carriage, closing his eyes, "you find Miss Hargreaves quite agreeable company and would prefer that anybody she was having tea with socially would go away."

Bryce Aiden Tyler defended his statement, "I am not jealous of Mr. Tweedbottom."

The carriage took a sharp turn and nearly ended up on two wheels. Then it landed with a THUNK.

At that moment, Mr. Bryce Aiden Tyler pointed as he looked out the window and thumped the roof to tell the carriage driver to stop.

Bryce exclaimed, "Do you see that? In the road, there?"

The carriage halted.

Bryce pointed to the ground. Magistrate Pinkney looked out Bryce's window. There was a carriage wheel on the road. The sun was setting. Some distance away, they saw what looked as if it could be the outline of an overturned carriage.

Bryce got out and inhaled. "Do you smell that?"

Magistrate Pinkney also inhaled deeply and then coughed, "Smoke... a fire..." Magistrate Pinkney looked up... "See there!"

Bryce followed the outstretched arm of the Magistrate to the sky to see small puffs of smoke billowing up into the sky as if emanating from a controlled camp fire.

"We must make haste if we are to catch the light from the setting sun," Bryce stated hurriedly as he bolted off, running in the direction of the smoke.

Magistrate Pinkney turned to the carriage driver and ordered, "Wait here." Then, Magistrate Pinkney sprinted to catch up to Bryce.

"You don't know where the smoke is coming from. It may be a tribe and they may wish to scalp you! Be careful man!" the Magistrate warned.

"Oh," Bryce glanced at Magistrate Pinkney as he kept his pace up, "I think I'll be fine. It looks like a distress signal. They may not be particular about who rescues them..."

"You cannot assume that!" Magistrate Pinkney insisted, "Do not be fool hearty."

Bryce, ignoring the warning of the magistrate, turned again toward the direction of the smoke.

Both the Magistrate and Bryce heard voices. Bryce froze as he cocked his head to listen and held up a hand indicating that the Magistrate should remain motionless.

Bryce whispered, "I detect a man's voice and... a woman... no two women talking..."

"What are they saying?" The magistrate whispered in reply.

Bryce shrugged, as he could not discern the words over the sound of crackling wood on fire. Bryce and Magistrate Pinkney peered through the brush and saw a tiny clearing.

There was an older Indian woman, a tall Indian man... and he heard two other voices, probably female or perhaps young boys?

From his vantage point, Bryce Aiden Tyler could not see who the other two were.

All he was able to discern was that the small group appeared to be sitting around a fire, burning the remains of what appeared to be an old carriage.

The Indian man reached down, picked up the wheel, kicked out the spokes and threw them one by one onto the fire.

Magistrate Pinkney stepped to the side, trying to peek through the dense shrubbery.

He broke a twig and then the tall Indian man looked sharply in his direction, placing a hand on the hilt of a knife, which rested around the Indian man's waist.

11 CHAPTER 98: (JUNE 1776)
Silversmith and Billy say good bye to Peter Timothy

Silversmith and Billy Dawes said good bye to Peter Timothy.

Peter Timothy approached the Inn at Meeting Town where Silversmith and Billy Dawes were lodging. He met them outside the Inn.

Billy spoke first, "Our mistress has not yet arrived."

Peter Timothy replied, "I have enjoyed meeting the two of you and my wife will be enthralled at our adventure. I am sorry my schedule does not allow me the luxury to await the arrival of your mistress, Jane Hargreaves. I must return to my cozy South Carolina colony and attend to the needs of the Gazette."

"We understand," Silversmith smiled as she curtsied.

"I would always welcome correspondence, should you wish to inform me about the progress of your mission," Peter Timothy shared as he bowed, "You may post any mail to me by addressing it to the South Carolina Gazette."

"I would be happy to write to you once Mr. Dawes and I and Miss Jane have settled on our future living quarters."

"Then, this is not a final good-bye, but simply a postponement," Peter Timothy smiled.

"Oh, no. If invited, I would be delighted to correspond in future." Silversmith affirmed.

Mr. Timothy bowed acknowledging her offer, "I look forward to your letter, Miss Silversmith. I do wish you much success in your mission."

Peter Timothy turned to leave, then looked over his shoulder at Billy Dawes, "Remember to read that book you purchased... it is filled with practical and useful insight." He winked and strolled away.

Billy turned to Silversmith, "Miss Jane is quite delayed. Are you certain we should have asked the innkeeper to prepare a room for her?"

"Quite sure," Silversmith confirmed, "She'll be here... if not today, then tomorrow. We simply must remain here and wait."

12 CHAPTER 99: (JUNE 1776) Bryce meets the burning carriage

While his red-coated driver waited at the carriage on the road, Magistrate Karl Pinkney and Bryce Aiden Tyler crouched in the darkness, trying to remain concealed by the brush as they spied on the small clearing of people burning the remains of carriage wheels.

Magistrate Pinkney leaned over to Bryce and whispered, "Do you think that savage there has captured these ladies and is holding them captive?"

Bryce replied at the same volume of speech, "There is a woman, there, in some manner of native dress, but they don't appear to be hostile. They simply are talking."

The magistrate stepped closer, "But they are burning a carriage. Perhaps that Indian fellow captured the women."

Bryce shrugged, "Or perhaps he is defending them?"

When the tall Indian fellow put his hand on the hilt of a knife and looked around, both Bryce and Magistrate Pinkney froze and ceased conversation. When the Indian man relaxed and let the palm of his hand slip away from his knife hilt, then resumed breaking up another wheel and throwing it on the fire, Bryce and the Magistrate relaxed.

"Bryce," Magistrate Pinkney whispered, "I believe it would be prudent if we were to run back to my carriage at this time and leave these people to their fire."

Bryce and Magistrate Pinkney turned around to depart, but as if he travelled silently, the tall raven- haired Indian fellow strode over to their exact hiding position and cleared the brush aside, revealing the two retreating men.

"Sirs!" The tall Indian fellow barked, "Are you seeking shelter with us or do you intend to harm us?"

Both Bryce Aiden Tyler and Magistrate Pinkney were caught by surprise, but neither could ascertain if the shock was from being suddenly found during a retreat, or that this natively-garbed tall Indian spoke perfect English.

"Shelter. Definitely shelter," Magistrate Pinkney sputtered, not expecting such eloquent speech from the native.

"There is room by the fire for you to join us," TallMan welcomed with a polite bow.

Such considerate manners, neither Bryce nor Magistrate Pinkney were expecting from this imposing figure.

Confused, both men hesitantly followed the Indian man as he gestured with a smile to join the others, who were sitting around the fire.

Both Magistrate Pinkney and Bryce Aiden Tyler exchanged glances to convey their mutual surprise as to why this savage comported himself with such a refined gentlemanly demeanor. He was gracious, considerate, and very well spoken. Yet, he did not wear a powdered wig, a tailored jacket, nor any buckles or bows on his shoes. Indeed, both Bryce and Karl Pinkney looked down and took note of his moccasins. His footwear seemed to be crafted as a sort of slipper one wore when they got out of bed. Nothing made sense.

As TallMan, Magistrate Karl Pinkney, and Bryce Aiden Tyler approached the fire, they noted an older woman dressed in a beige doe skin dress.

She was holding a stick into the fire.

On the end of this stick was the body of a rabbit. She was cooking food.

It appeared as if the roasting was completed because just as the three men approached the three women, the older woman holding the roasted rabbit, pulled a roasted leg off and handed it to one of the European women.

Bryce could not discern their faces in the flickering shadows.

Then, one European woman stepped into the light to accept the other leg of the rabbit. Her face was softly illuminated by the glow of the flickering flames.

Bryce exclaimed, "Jane?"

"Who is there?" Jane asked nervously, as she peered into the darkness, seeing only TallMan accompanied by two shadowy figures moving cautiously behind him.

Bryce quickened his pace and strode straight for a disheveled Jane Hargreaves, niece to his deceased business partner, Floyd Hargreaves. As he approached the fire, his features were made visible to Jane.

"Mr. Tyler!" Jane jumped forward, surprised to see him. "How is this that you are here?"

"I assume," Bryce started indicating the Indian gentleman, "That the smoke billowing from this site was some sort of signal. We saw it and investigated."

"And you... Mr. Pinkney?" Jane exclaimed when she saw the magistrate emerge from the shadows, "How is it I am to be honored by the presence of his Majesty's official? Did you have more questions for me regarding the death of my Uncle Floyd? Did you also bring your brother and the doctor?"

Magistrate Karl Pinkney replied with a smile, "No, Miss Hargreaves. I arranged for my carriage to seek you out, at the behest of Mr. Tyler. He was concerned for your safety. It is quite good fortune that we have found you," The Magistrate looked around, "All of you..."

Jane explained, "I was headed to Meeting Town since my maid and driver await for my arrival."

Eliza Lucas, now spoke up without being introduced, "We were all heading to Philadelphia, but some loathsome youths entertained themselves by creating mischievous sounds which scared our horses and hired carriage driver away, leaving us alone with a shattered vehicle."

Jane added, "We were completely deserted! I think we would have perished if it had not been for TallMan and his mother, Eunice, staying at our side to keep us safe from the unknown wilderness."

"Well," Magistrate Pinkney evaluated, "I'm not sure our carriage is large enough for all of you..."

Magistrate Pinkney looked over TallMan from head to toe as he continued, "At least not for all to fit inside the carriage, but perhaps if you would accompany us to the road where my driver awaits, we can see how we might accommodate what we can to take you all to Meeting Town."

"At this moment? Lead the way!" Eliza Lucas exclaimed as she quickly stepped over to the red coated Magistrate with a smile.

Bryce added, "I think leaving now would be appropriate. Would not every person here prefer an Inn's pillow to a rock?"

13 CHAPTER 100: (LATE JUNE 1776)
Button is Hidden

A while after Susanna Wright had challenged Button in her storage hut, she finally got his agreement to remain there in Meeting Town and help the cause.

In order to keep him safe, she had to keep him in that storage hut, but made certain to bring him blankets, food and water. Susanna Wright discovered, through her delicate inquiries, that there was a ship anchored at port. It was suspected, this particular vessel was to be used to transport slaves. Since this was not an illegal practice, all Susanna could do was wait until after it had departed before she felt confident that Button could safely walk the streets.

In the open air market, she spied Mr. Robert Livingston, the man who was selected to pen the thoughts of the other committee members.

Surreptitiously, she sidled up to him and asked, "Has the committee completed their thoughts?"

While looking at wares in the cart of the same vendor, which opened the door to the hidden tunnel to release Button and Susanna when their secret barn meeting was raided, Mr. Livingston replied, "I have penned my draft and sent a copy to that Dunlap printer. He assured me he could work with a German newspaper friend of his to have it translated. We will then have both an English copy and German version distributed."

"When," Susanna Wright asked, "Will that translation be complete? When will it arrive?"

Mr. Livingston replied while proffering a coin and purchasing an item on the cart to avoid suspicions, "The German translation should arrive by carriage before the next meeting of congress."

"Before anything is signed?" Susanna Wright asked.

"That is the plan," Mr. Livingston replied. "It is nearly July and we must act." A patrolling lobster back observed the two talking.

Susanna Wright took that as a cue to part ways abruptly. As if they had done this before, both Robert Livingston and Susanna Wright took a step away from each other to opposite ends of the cart. The vendor approached Susanna.

"The fellow you escaped with. Is he

safe?" The vendor asked in hushed tones.

"I have him in my storage hut until the slave ship departs," Susanna replied. The vendor then approached Robert Livingston with an item, "Sir?"

The vendor spoke clearly, "I've just this in. Would you be interested in adding this to your purchase today?"

Robert Livingston clearly replied, "Let me examine it."

The vendor approached Robert Livingston and as he handed the item to him, he saw out of the corner of his eye that the red coated official had temporarily looked away.

The vendor leaned closer to Robert Livingston and whispered, "The outspoken fellow is safe for now."

Robert Livingston replied, "We ought not to discuss. We cannot risk being overheard."

The vendor replied, "What next?"

Robert Livingston said loudly, "I will not buy this today. Perhaps another time, thank you." Then Robert Livingston leaned in and whispered, "Tell Miss Wright to have that Button fellow at the signing. He must be there. He may need to sign for Georgia if we do not find somebody else willing to represent that area."

Robert Livingston strode away and the vendor slowly walked back to where Susanna Wright was examining various items.

"Have you found anything to your liking?" The vendor asked loudly. He then whispered, "Prepare to transport Button to the signing."

Susanna whispered in reply, "I have three meetings scheduled which I must keep before moving him anywhere."

"What meetings?" the vendor asked in whisper.

Susanna looked around.

Before replying, Susanna took a deep breath then clearly said, "I am expecting copies of the document. I must coordinate with the campaign to develop indigo products here for export. I have agreed to meet with a woman who wishes to have audience with Benjamin Franklin on the same subject which devastated our hidden Button."

"Colonial slave raids?" The vendor asked.

"Yes," Susanna nodded, "But I also cannot risk moving Button until that ship departs."

The vendor whispered, "Do you think you will have time for all that before Congress meets?"

Susanna shrugged. She enunciated her verbal reply crisply with the intent of tricking any listening in to think she was replying to the vendor's first question. "Not today, perhaps I will buy later."

The vendor understood that Susanna intended to do as much as she could before that vessel departed.

14 CHAPTER 101: (JULY 1 1776)
Caught (1 week later)

The small coffee shop in Meeting Town was crowded with tiny tables and chairs, which did not accommodate the fashionably wide skirts, which Jane Hargreaves wore. Susana Wright's simply unadorned garb allowed her to easily slip into a chair at the one remaining table in the corner by the front window.

Smiling, Susanna Wright allowed Jane Hargreaves to take another chair with more space to accommodate her skirts.

Jane looked at Silversmith who was standing outside the coffee shop gazing onto the street. Earlier, Jane had asked Silversmith to meet her at the coffee shop to collect her after her meeting with Susanna Wright was concluded.

Susanna started the conversation after she had ordered coffee for the two of them. "I don't think I have ever tried coffee," Jane commented.

"Well, until we can start growing our own teas," Susanna Wright said, "I would like to encourage others to drink a different hot beverage. This place is where most men meet to conduct business meetings, so I felt it appropriate for our meeting."

Jane smiled as a cup of dark liquid was served to her, steaming in its pewter mug with a small cloth wrapped around the handle to prevent the drinkers from burning their palms as they gripped the cup. "I'm so glad you listened to my maid's pleas to meet with me, Miss Wright. I was delayed due to unforeseen roadside incidents."

Smiling, Susanna Wright said, "Your Miss Silversmith was quite convincing, but we didn't know when you would arrive. You see, it was fortunate that you were travelling with Miss Eliza Lucas as I must discuss business with her, as well."

Jane smiled as she stared at the cup of steaming black brew before her, uncertain how to approach it. "Yes. Indigo. Miss Lucas informed me of her plans to make Indigo a product to export and how she needed to discuss matters with you." Jane commented, "It is such good fortune that we are all lodging at the same Inn."

"Indeed," Susanna replied.

Jane knitted her brow as she mentioned, "I was noticing that all the guests at the inn appear to be... well, from many places, yet I did not see any natives. No Indians..."

"Oh," Susanna Wright added, "One can never tell if they are on your side or not and so most Innkeepers won't permit their lodgings. There is a home not far away which permits such boarders for a reasonable price."

"You see, I had two Indian travelling companions and I simply wondered where they might be lodging..." Jane's voice trailed off.

"You must speak up. It is rather noisy in here," Susanna Wright clipped the end of Jane's sentence and said loudly, "I don't mean to be rude, but your delayed arrival has frustrated some of my other plans. I have another matter of moving something from here to... to someplace else, which requires my full attention. Now then, shall we get straight to the matter at hand?" Susanna wright winced a bit as she sipped the bitter hot black brew.

Jane didn't know how to start, so looked down as she gathered her thoughts. The noise of the conversations around her was getting louder. Jane started to form her words, but then stopped uncertain how much to say or how loudly to say it.

Growing impatient, Susanna wright interjected, "Now, your maid, Silversmith, told me your Uncle Floyd died. Oh, and you also rescued a woman who had escaped from an Indian raid? Anyway, to honor your uncle's memory, you wish to complete his mission which was to halt the sale of people who had come to these shores as Colonists... to stop them being captured and sold at the slave market. So, Miss Hargreaves, do you wish me to request a man of influence, such as Benjamin Franklin, to ink something on parchment making the capture of Colonists and their subsequent sale as slaves illegal? Hmm?"

Startled, Jane nodded, "yes", as she raised her cup to her lips and inhaled this new coffee aroma. They were surrounded by a lively crowd actively conversing about trivial matters whilst sipping this dark caffeinated brew at tiny tables. Suddenly, a commotion made both Susanna and Jane crane their necks to discern what was afoot.

15 What Just Happened?

Unexpected events had occurred around the secret barn meeting and preconceived notions of who to trust were challenged. Meanwhile, Bryce Aiden Tyler leaves the Dunlap home after he gets the information he needs. A new friend of Button's, Susanna, shows him how to slip through the secret passages to underground networks to save lives. Meanwhile Polly continues to translate the document so that more people in these colonies could understand the sacrifices which they may need to make to keep their freedom in this new land. Meanwhile Bryce finds the carriage, wonders if his efforts were all for naught. Is he doing too little too late with too few resources? Can he make a difference at all?

16 Did You Know

Some who practiced medicine in the newly settled lands, did not always demand money as payment for their medical services. For example, Doctor Ebenezer Roby, who worked in the mid 1700s, accepted salted pork and rye in exchange for medical care. (Roby, Ebenezer, 1701-1772. Account book of Ebenezer Roby, 1749-1764 (inclusive). B MS b121, Countway Library of Medicine.)

In other colonies, doctors had recorded payments of: Linen handkerchief, brown sugar, butter, and a bushel of "Ingeon meal," (Peirce, D. (Daniel). Ledgers of Daniel Peirce, 1762-1809 (inclusive). B MS b131.1, Volume 1, Countway Library of Medicine.) There was no standardized system of care and each service had its own negotiation before payment was collected.

Old remedies were created. As far back as 1643, Massachusetts Bay Colony

Governor John Winthrop, a London doctor, treated gunpowder burns with a salve which contained "Mosse that groweth on an old thackt howse top." (For Burning with Gunnpowder or otherwise. Stafford, Ed. (Edward), 1617-. Receipts to cure various disorders for my worthy friend Mr. Winthrop, by Edward Stafford, 1643 May 6. B MS b76, Countway Library of Medicine.)

This would indicate that in the early 1600s, homes were built to allow a grass roof for insulation. In modern times, it has been found that grass or a green roof could absorb rain water and makes storm-water management easier. It also provides a home for wildlife. Some say the insulation with a grass roof keeps the temperature inside the home more consistent and regulated than traditional modern insulation. A grass roof may also reduce the modern shingle roof repair and maintenance needed because there are no shingles to fix. Some may keep a roof "mowed" by allowing goats to walk on the roof and graze.

16 VOCABULARY

Estate: A big piece of land with gardens and a grand fancy house.

Hypnotic / hypnotize: Keeps your attention. With hypnotic suggestion, a person can be made sleepy and then follows directions.

Unassuming: Shy, quiet, modest.

Volatile: Can change quickly, suddenly.

ABOUT Wynter Sommers

Wynter Sommers is the pseudonym for an American writing team, which harnesses multiple skills in technology, research, history and education. Formally trained with a PhD in Education, Wynter Sommers blends academic classroom experience, with corporate sophistication, and a passion for developing more effective student insights through engaging storytelling.

Wynter Sommers has a heart to inspire creativity and develop critical thinking skills, all to encourage readers to make wise choices in life.

Wynter Sommers takes each story and weaves the plot with classic gripping elements, which endure throughout repeated readings, revealing new meanings each time the story is explored. The small choices a reader makes in real life could have a lasting effect in future generations. This set of stories shows the origin of not just Bjorn Esterday and Sarah Paradise, but of their ancestors and the sort of world which was established, which unfolded in each generation until Bjorn and Sarah met.

It is rewarding to learn of heartfelt, thought provoking conversations taking place globally about the characters of these books. Should the reader be presented with extraordinary circumstances, it is the sincerest wish that they act with honor, truth and integrity to overcome obstacles in real life whilst the reader hones skills of self-reliance and collaborative teamwork despite barriers outside of the reader's control. Wynter Sommers hopes you enjoy the other **Bjorn Esterday Was not Born Yesterday** stories in this series.

117